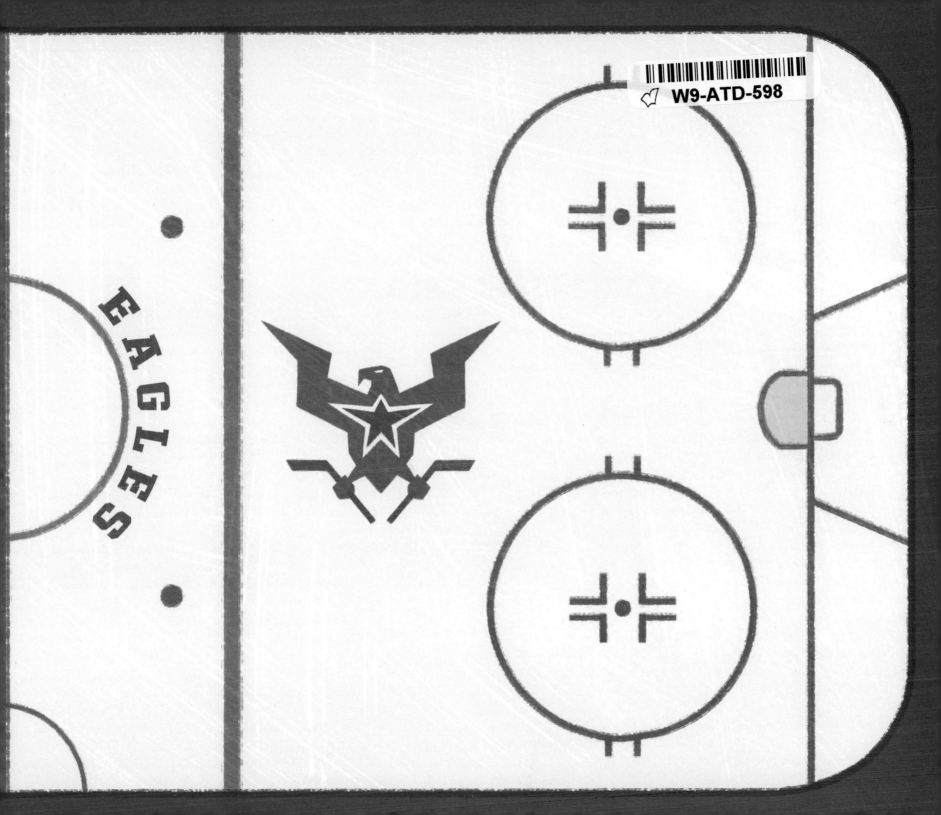

Sports Illustrated KIDS

GOODNIGHT HOCKEY

BY MICHAEL DAHL   ILLUSTRATED BY CHRISTINA FORSHAY

CAPSTONE
YOUNG READERS

In the heart of our town,
in the snow,
in the cold,

is the home of our heroes,
daring and bold.

We squeeze under blankets,
up in the stands,

mugs of hot chocolate
warm up our hands.

Here come the players!
They zoom and they glide!

They take center ice,
lining up on each side.

The puck drops — sticks and skaters collide!

A slapshot —
the puck sails out wide!

The players zig
and they zag.
The puck flies
like a rocket.

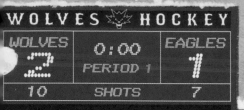

It's the end of the first,
lots of action and goals.

The Zamboni chug-chugs,
smoothing ice as it rolls.

The players take the ice.
Shots fly from each side.

WOLVES 🐺 HOCKEY

WOLVES	9:56	EAGLES
3	PERIOD 3	2
23	SHOTS	20

A stick swings — it's a hat trick!
The crowd jumps and cheers.

We throw our hats on the ice
and cover our ears!

One minute left —
where's the puck?
Will they score?

WOLVES 🐺 HOCKEY

WOLVES	0:00	EAGLES
3	PERIOD 3	2
30	SHOTS	24

The final buzzer sounds.
Our team wins!
We all ROAR!

It's a game to remember, but it's chilly and late.

We all say goodnight as we head toward the gate.

Goodnight, ice,
goodnight, ref.

Goodnight, stands,
and the fans who have left.

Goodnight,
moon,
and arena
aglow!

Goodnight, friends in their cars driving by.

Goodnight, stars in a wintry sky.

Goodnight,
Mom and Dad.

Goodnight, team.

Tonight is a
night for my own
hockey dream!

TO JOE ZIEGLER

Published by
CAPSTONE YOUNG READERS
a Capstone imprint
1710 Roe Crest Drive, North Mankato, Minnesota 56003
www.capstoneyoungreaders.com

Library of Congress Cataloging-in-Publication data is
available on the Library of Congress website.

ISBN: 978-1-62370-298-4 (hardcover)

Designer: Bob Lentz

Printed in the United States of American, in North Mankato.
112016   10118R